LUCY DANIELS

The Curious Kitten

Illustrated by Andy Ellis

To Sufi – another very curious puss!

Special thanks to Narinder Dhami

Little Animal Ark is a trademark of Working Partners Limited
Text copyright © 2001 Working Partners Limited
Created by Working Partners Limited, London, W6 0QT
Illustrations copyright © 2001 Andy Ellis

First published in Great Britain in 2001 by Hodder Children's Books

This edition published in 2007

A Catalogue record for this book is available from the
British Library

ISBN-13: 978 0 340 93251 3

Printed and bound in Great Britain by Clays Ltd, St Ives plc

Hodder Children's Books
A division of Hachette Children's Books
338 Euston Road, London NW1 3BH
An Hachette UK Company
www.hachette.co.uk

Chapter One

"Mum, where do tigers live?" Mandy Hope asked. She was pasting a picture of a tiger into her animal scrapbook.

It was the first day of the half-term holiday, and almost time for morning surgery at Animal Ark. Mandy's mum and dad were vets. The surgery where they worked was built onto the back of their cottage.

Mandy loved that. There were always plenty of animals around!

Emily Hope looked up from the pile of letters she was opening. "Well, there are tigers in Russia, and some in China – but India has the most tigers," she said. "They like to live in the jungle."

Mandy stuck the picture down carefully on the next blank page. "I'd *love* to go to India and see the tigers!" she sighed.

Her mum smiled. "One day, we'll go," she promised. "Your scrapbook's getting very full. We'll buy a new one when we go shopping."

"Great!" Mandy said happily.

She had collected *loads* of pictures.
She might even need *two* new
scrapbooks!

"Mandy?"

Mandy looked round.

Jean Knox, the Animal Ark
receptionist, had come into the
kitchen.

"There's someone in
the waiting-room
asking for you,"
Jean said, her eyes
twinkling.
"Who?"
Mandy
asked, jumping up.
"Your friend, Jill
Redfern," said Jean.

Mandy rushed into the
Animal Ark waiting-room.
It was quite crowded. It always
was on a Monday morning!

She spotted Jill sitting in
the corner. Her friend was with a
woman holding a large cat basket.

"Hi, Mandy," Jill said, waving

at her. "This is my aunt. She's brought her kitten in to get a microchip!"

"Hello, Mandy," Jill's aunt said, smiling. "I'm Sarah – and this is Shamrock."

Mandy smiled back, then
went over and peered into the cat
basket. Inside was a tabby kitten.

He had a fluffy golden brown
coat, striped with black – just like
a tiger! He was *very* cute.

"Hello, Shamrock!" Mandy said. Then she looked at Sarah. "He's gorgeous! But why have you called him Shamrock?" she asked.

Sarah smiled. "Look at his eyes," she said.

Mandy pushed her fingers through the wire. The kitten began to purr, and rubbed his head against Mandy's hand. Then he looked up at her with the greenest eyes Mandy had ever seen! As green as shamrock leaves.

Mandy grinned. "Good name!" she agreed. She laughed as Shamrock poked a fluffy paw through the wire, and tried to grab the sleeve of her sweatshirt.

"You told me all about microchips, Mandy, remember?" said Jill.

Mandy nodded. Microchips helped owners to find their pets when they were lost.

"Once Shamrock's chip is fitted, I'm going to let him out into the garden," Sarah said. "I've taken the week off work so that I can watch over him. He might be a bit scared out there, at first."

Just then, Mandy's dad, Adam Hope, looked into the waiting-room, and smiled. "I'm ready for Shamrock Redfern, now," he said.

Mandy grinned. Shamrock was trying to open the catch on the basket, pulling at it with his teeth as hard as he could. "And I think Shamrock's ready for *you*, Dad!"

Chapter Two

"Dad, can I come in and watch, please?" Mandy asked, as Sarah carried Shamrock into the examination room.

Mr Hope looked at Sarah.

Sarah smiled. "Of course," she said.

"He seems a lively little chap!" Mr Hope grinned as Shamrock tried again to pull the basket door open. "Let's get him out."

Mandy watched as her father undid the catch. Sometimes cats and kittens didn't want to come out onto the examining table. But straight away, Shamrock jumped out, looking around. Then he skidded towards the edge of the table, ready to explore.

"Oh, no, you don't," said Mr
Hope, grasping the kitten firmly.

Shamrock gave an unhappy
mew. He looked up at Mr Hope
with his big green eyes, as if to
say, *"Spoilsport!"*

Mandy and Jill burst out
laughing.

"He's into *everything*," Sarah said. "He's been in every cupboard in my house, and climbed up every curtain. He's just so nosy! And he's *always* trying to pull his collar and name-tag off!"

"Then it's a very good idea for him to have a microchip before he goes outside," Mr Hope said. He grinned as Shamrock tried to burrow up the sleeve of his white coat. "Just in case he forgets his way home!"

"Dad, I think Shamrock's got his head stuck!" Mandy pointed out. Shamrock was struggling to get out of Mr Hope's sleeve and mewing for help.

Mr Hope laughed, and rescued Shamrock. He handed the kitten to Sarah, and sorted through his equipment. "We use a needle to put the microchip in Shamrock's neck," he said.

"But it doesn't hurt," Mandy added, seeing Sarah and Jill look a bit worried. She'd watched her dad fit a tiny chip under a pet's skin before.

Her dad nodded. "Shamrock won't even know it's there," he said.

"So how does the microchip help find Shamrock if he gets lost?" Jill asked.

"The microchip has a number on it," Mr Hope said. "And the number is stored on a computer, with Sarah's address and phone number. So if someone finds Shamrock, a vet can read the number on his microchip, using a special machine, and find out who his owner is."

"That's great!" Sarah said. "But I'm still a bit worried about letting Shamrock outside. What if he runs off?"

"Well, when he first goes out into the garden, make sure that he's hungry," Mr Hope said. He prepared the needle. "Most kittens won't stray too far away from their next feed."

"Good idea!" said Sarah, looking happier. "Shamrock is always hungry. He uses up so much energy exploring everywhere!"

Jill turned to Mandy. "Would you like to come home with us and watch Shamrock go outside for the very first time?" she asked.

Mandy's face lit up. "I'd love to!" she beamed, tickling Shamrock's fat little tummy.

Chapter Three

"You're home, Shamrock," Mandy said, as she carried the kitten up to Sarah's front door. She and Jill had taken it in turns to carry the basket during the walk through Welford. "You'll soon be free again!"

Shamrock mewed loudly, and pawed crossly at the sides of the basket.

"He can't wait to get out!" Jill grinned. "Maybe he's hungry."

"He wants to get out and have a good nose round, you mean!" Sarah said, unlocking the door.

They all went into the kitchen.

Mandy put the cat basket down on the floor. "Shall I let Shamrock out?" she asked.

Sarah nodded. "I'll find some string," she said.

As soon as Mandy opened the basket, Shamrock jumped out.

He rushed over to her and Jill, purring loudly as they ruffled his fur. But after a few moments he dashed off again.

"Where's he going?" Jill asked.

"Look!" Mandy pointed across the kitchen. The door of Sarah's washing-machine was open, and Shamrock was standing on his back legs, peering inside.

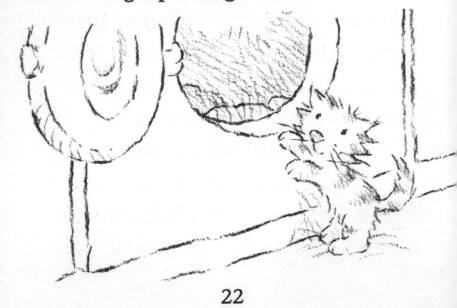

Mandy rushed over and grabbed the kitten just as he was about to jump in. "You're clean enough already, Shamrock," she laughed. The kitten didn't seem to agree. He sat down on the floor and began to wash himself with his tiny pink tongue.

Sarah sighed. "I'd better keep that door closed from now on," she said. Then she looked at her watch. "It's not quite time to take Shamrock out yet. Let's have a snack while we're waiting."

Mandy and Jill nodded.

"OK. Can I show Mandy the photos of Shamrock when he was really tiny, Sarah?" Jill asked.

Sarah smiled. "Sure," she said. "The album is next to the TV."

Jill and Mandy went off with their orange juice and chocolate biscuits to find it.

In the photos, Mandy saw that Shamrock was fluffier when he was a tiny kitten. But his coat was more tiger-stripy now. And she liked tiger stripes!

Afterwards, Mandy and Jill went to look for Shamrock. They found him in the kitchen. He'd finished his wash, and was sitting by his food bowl.

Sarah looked at her watch again and smiled. "Now it's time for Shamrock's next meal – and his rumbling tummy knows it!" she said.

She picked the kitten up and opened the back door. "All right, girls," she said. "Time to take him outside!"

Mandy looked around the back garden. It wasn't very big, so there weren't many places for Shamrock to hide. And the fences were too high for a kitten to jump over. There were no holes in them, either, for Shamrock to get through. He would be quite safe, she thought.

Shamrock was looking around too. He sniffed the air hard, and his eyes darted everywhere.

"Well, here goes!" said Sarah, sounding a bit nervous. She put

Shamrock gently down on the grass.

Mandy watched the kitten as he looked around his big new world.

Shamrock took a few careful steps over the lawn. A butterfly fluttered over his head, and he snapped playfully at it. Then he looked at Mandy and the others as if to say, *"Aren't I clever?"*

They all laughed, and Shamrock raced back to them, purring. He skidded to a halt, and then pounced on one of Mandy's shoelaces.

"Shamrock!" Sarah said, pretending to be cross.

The kitten ran off, tail waving madly. He ran as far as he could – until he reached the end of the lawn, when he was stopped by some bushes. Then he ran across the grass in the other direction – until the fence stopped him again.

"He doesn't seem at all scared of being outside," Mandy said.

"He loves it!" Jill laughed. Shamrock chased after a leaf that was dancing in the breeze. "Clever boy, Shamrock!" she called.

They watched Shamrock explore the garden for long time. He was having great fun. But every so often, he'd come bouncing back for a stroke and a cuddle.

"I think he's making sure we haven't left him on his own," Mandy said, grinning. She picked Shamrock up and he purred loudly.

"I'm so pleased that he's coming back to us and not trying to run off!" Sarah said. She seemed less worried now.

Before long, the kitten began to struggle in Mandy's arms. He wanted to get down again. Mandy put Shamrock back on the grass, and he bounded across the lawn, pouncing on daisies as he went.

Mandy beamed. The kitten was really enjoying himself!

Suddenly a blackbird flew overhead. It landed in one of the trees next to the garden fence.

Shamrock spotted it straight away. He raced over, and was up the trunk in a flash, digging his sharp little claws into the bark.

The blackbird
flew off in alarm.
"Shamrock!"
Sarah called.
"Come down!"
The kitten
wasn't listening.
He was climbing
further up the
tree. Moments
later, he was
level with the
top of the fence.
Mandy
gasped. "He
won't jump over,
will he?" she said
anxiously.

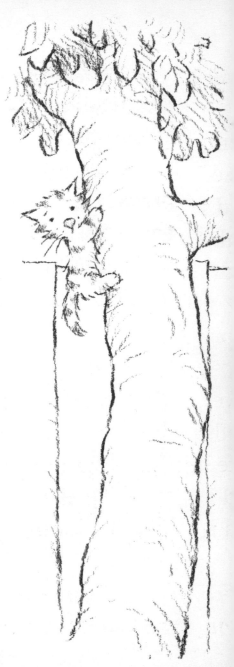

"No, it's much too high," Sarah said.

But Shamrock didn't seem to think so. He crawled out onto a branch level with the top of the fence.

Then he hopped onto the fence and disappeared over the other side. There was a loud scraping noise as the kitten clawed his way down the wooden fence post.

"Oh no!" Mandy cried.

Chapter Four

They all rushed over to the back gate.

Then Sarah groaned. "I forgot – it's locked!" she cried. "I'll get the key!" And she raced back inside.

Mandy's heart thumped. Jill looked worried too.

Suddenly Mandy remembered what her dad had said. "Food!" she yelled. "Sarah – he might come back for food!"

Sarah rushed back out into the garden. She had a key in one hand and a box of kitten biscuits in the other. Quickly she unlocked the gate, and they all rushed through.

They were in an alleyway. It ran behind the gardens then led out into the street in front of Sarah's house. But there was no sign of Shamrock.

Mandy's heart sank. If Shamrock had run out into the street, she just hoped he stayed away from the traffic.

They ran to the end of the alley.

"Shamrock! Come here, boy!" Sarah called. She shook the box of biscuits loudly.

But there was no sign of the kitten.

Mandy sighed. Even a rumbling tummy wasn't going to stop *this* curious kitten's adventure.

Peter Foster was walking by with his dad. Peter was in Mandy and Jill's class. He was walking his Cairn terrier pup, Timmy.

"Hi, Peter," Mandy said. She bent down to give Timmy a quick pat. The pup wagged his tail hard, then jumped up and licked Mandy's chin.

Mandy looked up at Peter. "We're looking for a tabby kitten," she said.

"You haven't seen one out here, have you, Peter?" Jill added.

"Sorry, no," Peter said. "And Timmy would have noticed a kitten running around. He tries to chase cats, I'm afraid!"

Peter and his dad wished them luck. They walked off with Timmy towards the village green.

"At least Shamrock's got his microchip," Mandy said. "*And* the name tag on his collar."

Jill looked a bit more cheerful. "You're right, Mandy," she agreed.

"Shall we search the front gardens in the street?" Mandy asked.

"Yes," said Sarah. "You two go one way, and I'll go the other." She looked very worried. "But don't cross the road, even if you see Shamrock on the other side," she warned. "Come and fetch me."

Mandy and Jill nodded, then set off down the street. They stopped at every gate and peered in. They just *had* to find Shamrock.

Then a flash of bright yellow in one of the gardens caught Mandy's eye. Something was hooked over one of the branches of a large, leafy bush.

She went over to see what it was. "It's Shamrock's collar!" she gasped.

Jill rushed to see. She nodded, her eyes wide. "It's definitely Shamrock's. That's Sarah's phone number on the name tag," she said. "It'll be even harder to find him now!"

"Thank goodness he has his microchip as well," Mandy said.

Jill ran to fetch her aunt, and the three of them searched the area where Mandy had found the collar. Sarah kept on shaking the box of kitten biscuits loudly.

They asked everyone they

met if they'd seen Shamrock. But they didn't find the missing kitten.

"Where *can* he be?" Jill said tearfully as they all stood outside Sarah's house, not knowing where else to look.

Just then, the Animal Ark Land-rover turned into the street.

"Here's my mum," Mandy said in a small voice. "It's time for me to go home."

Mrs Hope drew up at the kerb and climbed out. The smile on her face faded as she saw all the gloomy faces. "What on earth has happened?" she asked.

"Oh, Mum!" Mandy said in a wobbly voice. "Shamrock's disappeared, and no one knows *where* he is!"

Chapter Five

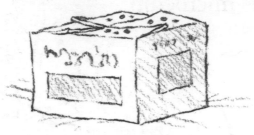

"Cheer up, love," Mrs Hope said, putting an arm around Mandy and giving her a hug.

Mandy and her mum were sitting in the Animal Ark living-room watching TV, while her dad took evening surgery. Mandy hadn't eaten much of her tea. She'd been too upset about Shamrock.

"I bet someone will find Shamrock and take him to the

local animal shelter," Mrs Hope added. "And he has a microchip now."

Mandy nodded. But it was getting dark. She couldn't bear to think of the little kitten out there, all on his own. Sarah had said she would telephone them as soon as Shamrock turned up. But the phone hadn't rung at all.

"Why don't you go and see what Dad is doing?" her mum said. "Seeing some other animals might stop you worrying for a bit."

"OK," Mandy said. She gave her mum a little smile, and went through into the Animal Ark waiting-room.

There was hardly anyone left in there now. Jean Knox was busy at her desk. A girl carrying a grey rabbit in a cage was paying her bill. The only other person there was a young man with a cardboard box on his lap.

Mandy could see that it wasn't a proper carrying-box,

just an old
supermarket
box with holes
punched in
the lid.

The man
saw Mandy
looking, and
grinned at her.
"Hi there."

"Hello," Mandy said shyly.
"What's in there?"

"A kitten," the man replied.
The sound of loud scratching
came from inside the box.

"Oh," Mandy said sadly,
thinking of Shamrock. "What's
wrong with it?"

The young man shrugged. "Well, nothing, as far as I know," he said. "I found it in my garden, eating some bacon rinds I'd put out for the birds. I didn't know where else to take it. It's not wearing a collar, so I'm hoping the vet can check for a microchip."

Mandy's eyes opened wide, and her heart beat faster. "Could I have a look, please?" she asked.

The young man nodded and opened up the cardboard flaps. A golden brown fluffy head, striped with black, popped out.

"Miaow!" the kitten said crossly.

"Shamrock!" Mandy cried.

She scooped the kitten up and hugged him hard. Shamrock rubbed his face against Mandy's, and began to purr happily.

"Oh, Shamrock!" Mandy whispered. "You're safe!"

She looked at the young man, who seemed rather surprised. Then she laughed. "You're right," she said. "My dad *can* check for a microchip – but there's no need to this time. *I* can tell you who this kitten belongs to!"

Chapter Six

"Hello?"

Mandy's heart beat faster when she heard Jill's voice at the other end of the line. "Jill, it's Mandy!" she cried. "I've found Shamrock!"

"What?" Jill gasped. "Sarah, Mandy's found Shamrock!"

"Oh, thank goodness!"

Mandy could hear Sarah hurrying down the hall.

"Where did she find him? Is he all right?"

Mandy grinned. She was still holding Shamrock, who was trying to jump down and  explore the waiting-room. "He's fine," she said. Then she explained exactly how the runaway kitten had been found.

"We'll be over to collect Shamrock right away," Sarah said, taking the phone from her niece. "And can you keep the person who found him there, so that we can say thank you?"

"OK," Mandy said happily. She put the phone down. Her mum and dad had both come out to the waiting-room to see what was going on. They were talking to the young man who'd brought Shamrock in, and smiling. "Sarah and Jill are on their way," Mandy told them. She turned to the man. "And they'd like you to wait, so that they can thank you."

The man looked rather embarrassed. "I ought to be getting off home—" he began.

Mrs Hope shook her head firmly. "Jill and her aunt will want to thank you properly, Mr . . ."

"Smith," the man said. "But call me Jonathan."

"Yes, you really must stay, Jonathan," agreed Mr Hope. "If it wasn't for you, Shamrock might still be lost! Come into the kitchen for a cup of tea while we wait."

*

"I wonder if this tiny fellow *is* microchipped," Jonathan said, as he sat in the Animal Ark kitchen. Shamrock had jumped onto his lap, and was having his tummy tickled. "He certainly *should* be if he's so curious!"

Mr Hope nodded and grinned. "The little rascal was microchipped just this morning. I did it myself!"

"So you must like it here, Shamrock," Jonathan joked. "Two visits in one day!"

Shamrock then began to struggle to get down to do more exploring. He disappeared under the kitchen table.

"Fetch the biscuit tin, would you, love?" Mr Hope said to Mandy.

Mandy nodded. When she came back from the pantry with the tin, she took a bite from a chocolate chip cookie. Then she crawled under the table to see what Shamrock was up to.

But there was no sign of him.

"Shamrock!" she called. "Where have you gone this time?"

"I hope he hasn't got lost again," Jonathan said, as he sipped his tea.

"He can't be far away," said Mandy.

Just then, the doorbell rang. Mandy put her half-eaten cookie on the table and raced to the door. "Here they are!" she yelled.

Jill and her aunt were standing outside, beaming all over their faces.

"Where's that naughty kitten of mine?" Sarah asked.

"In the kitchen," Mandy replied. "But we're not sure exactly where," she said under her breath.

Sarah and Jill followed Mandy back into the kitchen.

After smiling hello to Mr and Mrs Hope, Sarah turned to Jonathan. "Thank you *so* much for bringing Shamrock here. It was certainly the right place!" she said, beaming.

"It was no trouble – you're welcome," said Jonathan, smiling back.

Sarah looked around. "So where is he?" she asked.

Mr Hope coughed. "Er, he's here *somewhere*," he said. "He's gone off exploring again." Everyone laughed.

Suddenly a scrabbling noise made them jump. A moment later, Shamrock squeezed out from behind the cooker, looking rather grubby and dusty and miaowing at the top of his voice.

"Shamrock!" Sarah quickly scooped him up. "You bad, bad boy!" she said, giving him a hug.

"He must have come out to see why we're all laughing," Mandy said, scratching the top of Shamrock's furry head. "Shamrock, you really are a curious kitten!"

Shamrock mewed loudly as if he quite agreed.

Chapter One

"We're not late, are we, Dad?" Mandy Hope asked. "Amy will be waiting for me."

It was Saturday morning and Mr Hope was taking Mandy to her friend Amy Fenton's house.

Mr Hope smiled as he drove past Welford village green. "Don't worry, love," he said. "The pet shop won't run out of mice before you and Amy get there!"

"I know, Dad," Mandy said with a grin. "But we want to get there early. Amy says it's going to take ages to find just the right mouse!"

Mandy loved animals. Her mum and dad were both vets.

There were always animals around at Animal Ark, their surgery. Today, Amy was going to buy a pet mouse. She'd asked Mandy to come and help her choose.

"Make sure you and Amy look for a healthy mouse, won't you, Mandy?" said Mr Hope, as they pulled up outside Amy's house.

"Yes, Dad," she said. "What should we look out for?"

"Well, a healthy mouse will have nice bright eyes, and clean fur," said Mr Hope. "Has Amy bought a cage for the mouse yet?"

Mandy shook her head. "No, she's buying *everything* today."